THE NITE-GLO GANG

GO EXPLORING

Pictures by David Mostyn

Based on original characters by Steve McLaughlin

PICTURE CORGI

One blowy, blustery day, the Gang went down to the beach. It was too cold to swim so they decided to play a game.

'We can be explorers,' said Osmo. 'Let's see who can find the best thing on the beach.'

'Perhaps we'll find some treasure!' said Wim, the smallest one.

'I don't think that's very likely,' laughed Osmo. 'But there will be a special prize for the winner at tea-time.'

'What fun!' said Kandy. 'Let's go!'

Beeny and Pod found a lot of small pools with strange plants and animals in them. At the bottom of one pool, Pod found a beautiful shell. When he held it to his ear, he could hear the sound of the sea.

Osmo and Cam found four kinds of seaweed. There was
a brown bubbly one, a thin green wispy one, a black
knobbly one and a big leafy brown one. They were
all very slimy!

Kandy and Fing found a starfish.
    'Perhaps it fell from the sky at night,' said Fing.

Wim and Hamish didn't have much luck. They found
a sand castle.

'We can't take that back,' said Hamish.

They found a huge lump of driftwood buried in the
sand. It was too heavy to move.

They found a boat pulled up on the shore. It
belonged to somebody else.

Then they found a cave.

The cave was very big and dark.

'I don't think we ought to go in there,' said Hamish.

'Oh, pooh!' said Wim. 'I'm not afraid of anything.'

'Come on, Wim, you can't go exploring in there. You're only little and you haven't even learned to glow yet!'

'Oh, pooh!' said Wim as he marched into the cave.

Inside, the cave got darker and darker. Sometimes Wim thought he saw a glint in the dark, sometimes he thought he heard a strange noise. Then, all of a sudden, there was a terrible rumbling, like a monster's tummy, and a huge pile of rocks came tumbling down.

'Ooh-er! Help! I'm stuck!' cried Wim. But he had gone too far into the cave. There was no-one to hear him!

Hamish ran back to where the others were waiting to have tea.

'Wim's trapped in a cave!' he gasped.

They all rushed to the cave and began to search for Wim. Where could he be? How could they find him in the dark? If only he could glow . . .

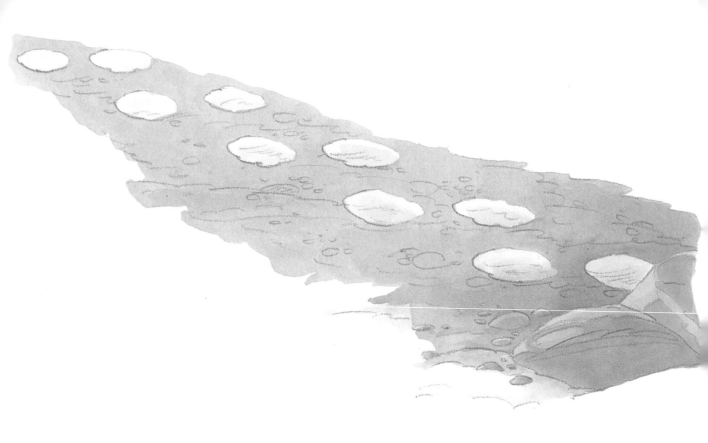

Then, deep in the twisty-wisty paths of the cave,
Hamish found some glowing footprints.

'Wim, where are you?' shouted Hamish.

'Here!' came a faint cry. 'Get me out!'

At tea-time, the Gang showed what they had found in the exploring game. There were all sorts of things. There were seashells and seaweed, starfish and cuttlefish, feathers and driftwood, and lots of stories. Everyone had something to show. Everyone, that is, except Wim and Hamish.

'Well, Wim,' said Osmo. 'What about you? Did you find your treasure?'

Wim looked sad.

'No. I didn't find anything. Nor did Hamish.'

'Oh, yes I did,' said Hamish. 'I found you!'

'And that has to win the prize!' laughed Osmo.